W9-BLH-520

WALT DISNEY'S

Gulliver Mickey

Random House 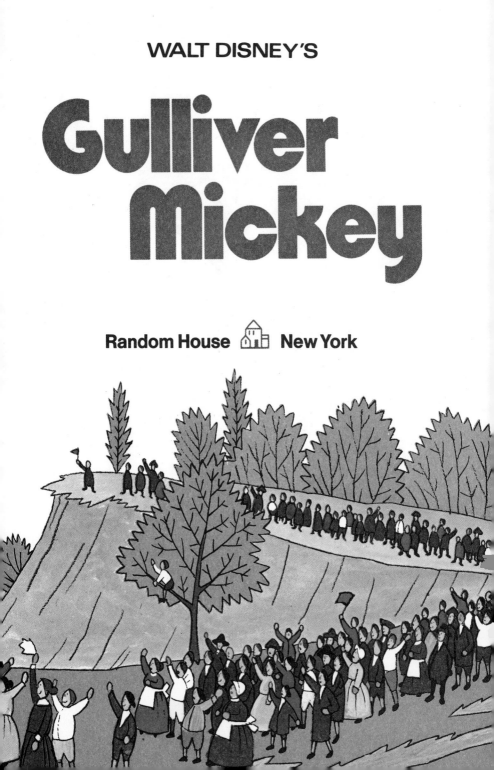 **New York**

Copyright © 1975 by Walt Disney Productions. All rights reserved under International and Pan-American Copyright Conventions. Published in the United States by Random House, Inc., New York, and simultaneously in Canada by Random House of Canada Limited, Toronto.
Library of Congress Cataloging in Publication Data
Main entry under title: Walt Disney's Gulliver Mickey. (Disney's wonderful world of reading, #27) Gulliver Mickey is shipwrecked in Lilliput, a land of tiny people, who, after they lose their initial fear of him, become his fast friends. [1. Fantasy] I. Disney (Walt) Productions. II. Title: Gulliver Mickey. PZ7.W168983 [E] 74-23399 ISBN 0-394-82561-6 ISBN 0-394-92561-0 (lib. bdg.)
Manufactured in the United States of America 0

BOOK CLUB EDITION

G H I J K

R

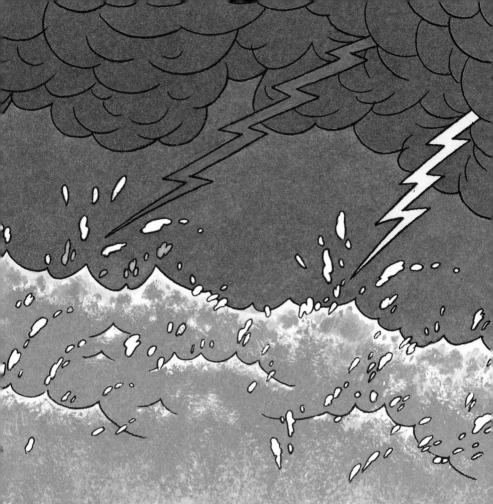

One night Gulliver Mickey was at sea
in his little sailboat.

Suddenly a terrible storm struck.

Giant waves washed over the boat.

Lightning flashed across the sky.

Thunder roared—BOOM! CRASH!

All at once a huge wave swept over the boat.
It tossed Mickey high into the air,
and threw him across the water.

The next thing he knew, he was rolling
head over heels on a sandy beach.

By this time Mickey was so tired
he fell asleep in the wet sand.

When Mickey opened his eyes the next mornin
he did not know where he was.

He tried to sit up, but he could not move.

"I must be dreaming," thought Mickey.

He wiggled his arms.
They were tied to the ground by tiny ropes.
He wiggled his legs.
They were tied to the ground, too.

Then Mickey turned his head to look around.

An army of tiny soldiers was marching toward him.

Some sat on tiny horses and carried tiny swords.

Others were pulling little cannons over the sand.

A few of the soldiers crept right up to Mickey.
They crawled into his pockets and
pulled out his watch.

They pulled out his pocketknife.

Then they opened his watch.
"Help!" cried a little old man
whose beard had caught in the wheels.

The soldiers had to chop off
his long white beard.

Now Mickey wiggled as hard as he could.
The tiny ropes broke and he sat up.

All at once a hundred tiny cannonballs
hit his chest—PING! PING!

But they were too small to hurt Mickey.

They bounced off his chest and rolled back
to the soldiers.

A fat little man on a fine brown horse began
to shout, "Load the cannons and fire again!"

"That must be the leader," thought Mickey.

He lifted him right off the ground, horse and all.

The angry little man pulled out his sword.
"Put me down this minute!" he said.
"I am the emperor of Lilliput."

Mickey smiled at the tiny emperor.

"Don't be afraid of me, Your Highness," said Mickey. "I do not want to hurt you."

Then he told the emperor about the storm that had blown him to Lilliput.

"All I want now," he said, "is something to eat."

Mickey put the little man back on the ground.

"Bring food for the giant!" the emperor shouted.

"He will not hurt us. He is a friend."

The little soldiers hurried away.

They knocked on every door in Lilliput.

"A giant has landed on the beach," they cried.

"Bring all the food you can spare!"

Soon the Lilliputians came with food
for Mickey.

They brought wagons full of cheese
and baskets of bread.

They had carts filled with fruit
and barrels of milk.

Mickey scooped up all the food
as the people passed by.

He ate everything.

At first the children were afraid of Mickey.
But they soon found out that he was a friend.
Mickey played with the children every day.

They made seesaws across his shoes and
played leapfrog over his fingers.

They played hide-and-seek in his pockets.

They climbed up to his knees
and slid down his legs.

One morning Mickey went to the beach
to sit by himself and think.

He had been in Lilliput for many weeks.
And the Lilliputians were very kind to him.
Still, Mickey was lonely.

He thought of his own home far across the sea.
He thought about all his old friends.
"How I wish I could see them again," he said.

Suddenly there was a shout.
"Ahoy!" cried the lookout
on the castle tower. "Enemy boats—
headed this way!"

The emperor's soldiers got busy at once.

Some of them jumped on their horses and
pulled out their swords.

Others rolled out the cannons and loaded them.

Mickey heard the shouting.
"Let me help!" he cried.
And he waded out to meet
the enemy boats.

The little boats came closer and closer.

They began to fire their cannons.

PING! PING! The tiny cannonballs
bounced off Mickey's chest.

Mickey took a deep, deep breath.

Then, with all his might...WHOOSH!
He blew the enemy boats right out of sight.

When Mickey came back the Lilliputians cheered.
"You have saved our country," said the emperor.
"Now we must do something for you. What do you
want more than anything else in the world?"

"You have all been very kind to me," said Mickey.
"But still I miss my own country. More than
anything else I want to go home."

"Perhaps we can help you,"
said the emperor.

For two whole days the Lilliputians worked.
They chopped down trees and dragged them
to the beach.

They mended ropes.

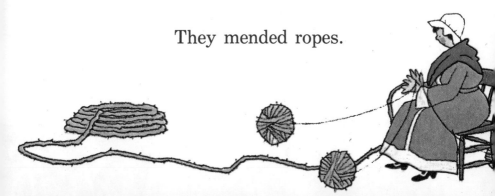

They split logs.

They hammered and measured
and sawed.

They sewed dozens of sheets together to make a giant sail.

Then they put the sail on a long pole and raised it high into the air.

When they were all done, they showed Mickey
what they had built for him.

It was a raft!

Now he had a way to get home again.

"Oh, thank you," said Mickey.

The Lilliputians filled their rowboats with barrels of food and water.

They loaded everything onto the raft
and Mickey climbed aboard.

The tiny emperor stood on the shore.
"We will miss Mickey," he thought.

As Gulliver Mickey sailed out to sea,
he waved good-by to the Lilliputians.

He was sorry to leave his new friends.

But he was happy to be on his way home at last.